Annie and the Kidnappers

Annie and the Kidnappers

By Amy Ehrlich

Illustrated by Leonard Shortall

Random House

To my father, a master storyteller
A.E.

 Published in the United States by Random House, Inc., New York, and simultaneously in Canada by Random House of Canada Limited, Toronto.

Library of Congress Cataloging in Publication Data:
Ehrlich, Amy, 1942–
Annie and the kidnappers.
SUMMARY: When she goes to a poor neighborhood to claim her missing dog, Sandy, Annie falls into the hands of kidnappers who demand a million dollars ransom from Daddy Warbucks.
[1. Kidnapping–Fiction. 2. Orphans–Fiction] I. Shortall, Leonard W., ill. II. Starr, Leonard. III. Title. PZ7.E328Al [Fic] 82-3697 AACR2
ISBN: 0-394-85413-6 (trade); 0-394-95413-0 (lib. bdg.)
Manufactured in the United States of America 2 3 4 5 6 7 8 9 0

Contents

1
Missing!

It was nine o'clock in the evening. Daddy Warbucks' mansion on Fifth Avenue in New York City was lit up like a Christmas tree. In the library the famous billionaire and his adopted daughter, Annie, were playing their nightly game of checkers. Between them sat Annie's dog, Sandy. His ears were cocked, and his eyes followed every move.

The game was almost over. Suddenly Annie moved her king and jumped Daddy Warbucks' last three men in one sweep. "Arf, arf!" barked Sandy. He jumped up and licked her face.

"Gee, Sandy, I didn't know you were rooting for me," said Annie. "You're the best friend a girl ever had."

Daddy Warbucks looked at Annie fondly and patted Sandy's head. "Yes," he said, almost to himself, "that dog's worth his weight in gold."

Annie yawned and began to put the checkers away. "Bedtime, Annie," said Daddy Warbucks.

"Do I have to?" she asked. But actually Annie didn't mind going to bed. She liked it when Daddy Warbucks told her a story and tucked her in. And when he left the room, she had Sandy to keep her company. He slept by her side all night, and his sweet, shaggy face was the first thing she saw when she opened her eyes each morning.

Sunlight streamed into Annie's bedroom. She threw back the covers and sat bolt upright. Something was wrong. She could feel it. "Sandy, are you there?" she whispered urgently. But even before she said it, Annie knew that Sandy was gone.

She got dressed quickly and ran into the hall. No one else was awake yet. Her footsteps rang on the marble floors. In a panic Annie checked room after room. Nothing! It wasn't like Sandy to wander off. Maybe he was sick or hurt.

Annie's heart was pounding. "Sandy, Sandy," she called. She raced down the stairs and out the back door. Dew sparkled on the lawn, and the spring morning was clear and fresh. But Annie hardly noticed. She had only one thought. She had to find Sandy. She just had to!

She dashed around wildly. In the garage the Rolls-Royce gleamed in the dimness, but Sandy was not there. The tennis courts were rolled smooth, but she saw no paw prints in the red clay. She even thought of looking inside Daddy Warbucks' private autocopter. Then she realized that Sandy could not possibly open the hatch.

What if he had wandered out into the street? He could get hit by a car! Annie gasped in fright. She rushed to the great iron gate at the driveway and unlatched it with shaking fingers.

Suddenly she heard someone call her name. Annie whirled around. Punjab,

Daddy Warbucks' Indian bodyguard, towered above her.

"You mustn't leave the mansion alone, little one. The master has said so many times." Punjab was smiling and his voice was soft, yet there was a warning in the words.

"I don't want to disobey, Punjab, honest I don't. But Sandy's missing and I gotta find him. Anyway, I know how to get around this whole city. I've been on my own before. Nothing bad's ever happened to me."

Punjab knelt in the grass beside Annie and took her hand. "That is true, little one. But you must remember that you are no longer an orphan. You are a rich man's daughter now, and there are many evil and greedy people in the world. Come, Mr. Warbucks will be worried."

They went to the dining room, where Daddy Warbucks was eating breakfast. He put down his coffee cup and stared hard at Annie. "Is something the matter, my dear?"

Hearing the concern in his voice, seeing his kind, familiar face, Annie finally lost control. She'd been trying to be brave for Sandy's sake, but now her fears overwhelmed her. She flung herself onto Daddy Warbucks' lap, sobbing so much she could not talk.

"If you please, sir. . . ." said Punjab. He quietly explained how he had found Annie at the front gate ready to go after Sandy.

"Can't you do something, Daddy? He's out there somewhere. I just know he is," Annie cried.

Daddy Warbucks took her by the shoulders and wiped her tears away with a big white handkerchief. "Now, now, we'll get Sandy back. Trust me, Annie. I love that dog as much as you do." He hurried over to the phone.

"Operator, this is Oliver Warbucks. Get me the dog pound. Then I want to speak to the chief of police, the mayor, and to every newspaper in the city. I have no time to waste.

"Hello, is this the pound? I'm looking for a shaggy brown dog. Answers to the name of Sandy. Has a red leather collar.

"You say you've got three shaggy brown dogs with red leather collars there? Size? I don't know. Maybe three feet tall. Oh, blast! Do I need to draw you a picture?

"Pictures! That's it!" Daddy Warbucks slammed the receiver down and started to pull out the drawers in his desk. "Ah, here they are! Remember these, Annie? We took them at your birthday party." He jammed his hat on his head and rushed to the door.

"I'll go run these photographs over to the newspapers. Sandy's picture will be on every street corner in New York City." He grabbed Annie and gave her a fierce hug. "Promise me you'll stay here with Punjab till I get back. The streets are dangerous, Annie. There are crooks and con men out there who'd sell their own mothers to make a dollar. Don't worry. We'll have Sandy back by nightfall."

Nightfall! Anything could happen to Sandy by that time! Annie had never felt so useless. She clasped her hands behind her back and began to pace the living room. That was what Daddy Warbucks always did when he was troubled. But she doubted it would help.

Punjab watched her for a time. Then he took out his yoga mat and unrolled it in the corner. Every morning he did Indian exercises, twisting himself into a series of pretzel shapes.

Suddenly the phone rang. Annie rushed to answer it. "Hello," she said, her voice shaking a little.

"Why, hello, dearie," said a warm, mothcrly voicc. "This is Mrs. Jiggs, thc milkman's wife. Early this a.m., when my hubby was by your house delivering the milk, a dog came out and chased his truck. Why, that dog just kept comin' after him all along the route, waggin' his tail like crazy, wantin' to play."

Annie listened but said nothing. Could it really be Sandy? It was hard to believe he'd go off with a stranger.

The woman rambled on. "Well, finally my hubby, he decided to take the dog and bring him home. He was afraid the dog would get lost, you see. So, dearie, your dog's with us. I got two sick kids at home, and my hubby, he's comin' down with it too. I had to run to the corner to make this call. So it would be best if you could come pick up the dog. He's right here. He wants to talk to you."

"Arf! Arf, arf!" It was Sandy's bark. No other dog in the world sounded like that. All of Annie's doubts melted away. Her heart raced with joy. In that split second nothing else mattered. She had decided to go get Sandy—by herself.

She glanced at the corner of the room. Good. Now Punjab was standing on his head with his legs crossed in midair. He could stay that way for hours. He claimed it helped him think clearly.

"What is the address?" she asked, trying to sound like Daddy Warbucks' secretary. If Punjab could hear her, she didn't want him to suspect that the call had anything to do with Sandy.

"It's 317 East Seventeenth Street," said the woman.

"Very good," said Annie. The numbers were stamped forever on her brain. She heard the receiver click. "Yes," she told the dial tone, "I'll give Mr. Warbucks the message."

Punjab still hadn't moved. Annie was certain he'd noticed nothing. She felt guilty about fooling him and breaking her promise to Daddy Warbucks. But it was all for Sandy's sake. Later on, after she'd brought him home, she'd explain everything. She was sure they would understand.

Annie went upstairs to keep clear of Punjab. Shc hadn’t yct figurcd out how to leave the house without being seen. But as she passed the room where the linens were kept Annie suddenly had an idea. She opened a cupboard and tied three of Daddy Warbucks’ monogrammed sheets together. Then she tiptoed into his office and fastened one end to a big chair near the window and threw the other end outside.

“Just stay upside down for three more minutes, Punjab, that’s all I ask,” thought Annie. This was it, the getaway. She slid down the sheets. Then she hit the ground and took off running.

“Be patient, Sandy. I’m coming!” Annie said. But the warm spring wind blew the words away, and there was nobody around to hear them.

2

317 East Seventeenth Street

Annie unlatched the iron gate and headed downtown. It felt great to be on the streets alone. She thought of the time she'd run away from the orphanage. What an adventure that had been! Of course, she wouldn't trade being Daddy Warbucks' daughter for anything in the world, but sometimes Annie missed her freedom. Since she'd come to live with him, she wasn't allowed to walk Sandy or go to the library or even get an egg cream unless a grownup came with her.

Annie knew that Daddy Warbucks worried only because he loved her. But there was nothing for him to be afraid of. No one was going to hurt her. She looked around. The only people she saw were an old woman walking a poodle and a doorman polishing the brass decorations on his building.

Farther up Fifth Avenue a fleet of double-decker buses was coming. Annie dug into her dress pocket. She had plenty of change. She raced to the nearest bus stop and swung onto a bus. She figured she'd go get Sandy and then take a cab back home with him. Punjab could pay the driver when they got there. Why, it'd be such a quick trip he'd never even miss her.

Annie climbed the stairs to the top of the bus. It was wonderful to be among people—old people, young people, rich and poor. Usually when she traveled now

it was in the Rolls-Royce with Daddy Warbucks' chauffeur. This was much more fun.

It was still early in the day, and there was little traffic. The bus moved rapidly down Fifth Avenue. At Seventeenth Street Annie pulled the bell cord and got off. She started to walk east. She figured it would be about six blocks.

The neighborhood she'd landed in was not so great. Instead of the big mansions and apartment houses near Daddy Warbucks' house, there were tenement buildings grimy with soot. Ragged children played in the street, and grownups sat sullenly on stoops as if they had no work to do and nothing to care about. It seemed to Annie that they were all staring at her. She looked down at her patent-leather shoes and her fancy red dress. For the first time she felt a little nervous.

As she walked through a group of girls who were playing jump rope, they pointed at her and laughed. "What're you doin' here, kid?" one of them yelled. "This isn't where you belong. Go back to your rich neighborhood!"

Annie could not stand being jeered at. If these girls thought she was some rich little sissy, they'd better think again! She stopped short and put her hands on her hips. "Rich neighborhood! If you really wanna know, I grew up in an orphanage down on Hudson Street. I bet I can run as fast as you, throw a ball as far as you, and play jump rope just as good."

The biggest girl in the bunch stuck her face only inches away from Annie's. "Oh, yeah?" she said threateningly. "You wanna prove it?"

"Well, actually I'm in kind of a hurry. . . ." said Annie.

The girl ignored her. "Clara, go get the other jump rope. We'll try this princess out on double dutch."

A little dark-haired girl stepped forward with a piece of clothesline. She glanced at Annie curiously and then handed the clothesline to the leader.

Annie was very aware of all the time this was wasting. But if the girls ganged up on her, it would only take longer to get to Sandy, and she didn't want that.

The two jump ropes slapped against the pavement in the old familiar rhythm. Back at the orphanage double dutch had been Annie's specialty. She just hoped her feet would remember how to move.

No problem! It was as easy as ever! For an instant Annie forgot that Sandy was waiting. She forgot about Punjab discovering she was gone. She was aware only of the ropes twirling and of her feet flashing in and out. The ropes went faster and faster, but Annie did not falter once. Then abruptly the game was over.

The two girls holding the jump ropes stepped aside to let Annie pass. No one looked her in the face or said a word, but as Annie walked away down the street, she had the feeling she was being followed. When she was almost at the entrance of 317 East Seventeenth Street, she whirled around. There stood the little dark-haired girl they had called Clara. She smiled at Annie shyly. "You were great!" she said. *"They'd* never admit it, but I just wanted you to know."

"Gee, thanks," said Annie.

"Wanna play sometime?" asked Clara. "You could come over to my house."

"Actually I don't live near here. I'm just picking up my dog." Annie turned to check the address of the building. It only took an instant, but when she turned around to say good-bye, Clara had already vanished.

"Too bad. She's a really nice kid," thought Annie, "and it seems like she could use a friend." But Annie couldn't worry about that now—Sandy was waiting. She turned her attention to the building in front of her. It looked neglected, almost unlived in. Many of the windows were boarded up, and the front door was covered with sheet metal. Could this really be the place?

Slowly she went inside. The hallway was so badly lit that at first Annie couldn't see anything. For a moment her courage left her, and she thought of turning back. Then faintly, from the top of the stairs, she heard Sandy barking. Annie shrugged off her fears.

What did it matter what a place looked like? It was the people who lived inside that counted. The Jiggses were probably so poor they couldn't afford anything better; she guessed milkmen didn't make much money. Maybe Daddy Warbucks would give them a reward for taking care of Sandy. Hey, that was a swell idea! She'd talk to him about it as soon as she got home.

Second floor, third floor, fourth floor. As Annie climbed the stairs Sandy's barking kept getting louder and louder. She could not wait to throw her arms around him. It seemed like forever since she'd seen him.

There was only one apartment on the top floor. Annie rang the bell. "Sandy, it's me!" she told her dog, almost jumping up and down with excitement. The door opened, and Annie walked inside.

She just had time to take in a poorly furnished room with a bare bulb overhead and newspapers pasted over the windows. Sandy was chained to the sink. On the table was a telephone. But wait—why had Mrs. Jiggs had to go to the corner to call? It was Annie's last thought. Just then someone hit her violently from behind, and she fell to the floor. Blackness closed in all around her.

Annie felt a warm, wet tongue on her face. She opened her eyes slowly. Her head throbbed. At first she had no idea where she was. Then she saw Sandy, and it all came back to her. She opened her mouth to scream, but no sound came out. She tried to leap up, but she could not move. Panic blotted out her thoughts. "Take it easy," she warned herself sternly. "Try to figure out what's going on here."

She looked down. She was sitting in a wooden kitchen chair. Her arms were tied behind her, and her ankles were tied to the chair legs. Sandy sat anxiously at her feet, wagging his tail and whimpering. There was a gag in her mouth, tied so tightly that it cut into her cheeks.

The room was empty and silent. Who had done this to her? And how was she going to escape? Annie shifted her weight

and tried to stand up, but the chair came with her. She bumped across the floor, scraping it behind her. At the door she lowered her head to the keyhole, but all she saw was the green wall across the hallway.

She'd need her hands free to get anywhere. All at once Annie had an idea. Maybe Sandy could chew the ropes off her wrists. He was a smart dog. There had to be a way she could make him understand. "Mmmph, mmmph!" she said commandingly, throwing her head back and looking toward her hands.

Sandy walked around behind her. "Arf!" he barked, pleased to hear Annie's voice. He put his head down on her wrists.

"That's it, Sandy!" she cheered him on in her thoughts. Annie moved her jaw up and down to show that she wanted him to bite the ropes. For a moment he looked puzzled. Then he opened his mouth and gently began to chew at the ropes. By craning her neck, Annie could tell he was making progress. She stretched her wrists wide to help him. With a ripping sound the ropes finally came apart.

Annie rubbed her wrists. The rope had cut into them, and they stung like crazy. But she couldn't stop to feel sorry for herself. She tore off the gag and began to work at the knots on her ankles. Golly, they'd tied them tight!

There! Annie stood up and nearly crumpled to the floor. Her legs were stiff and tingly. For the first time she wondered how long she'd been there. She glanced around. No light came through the torn newspapers covering the windows. It must be late—maybe even the middle of the night. Oh, why had she ever disobeyed Daddy Warbucks! He'd be frantic with worry.

There wasn't a moment to lose. She had to get away. Whoever had done this to her could come back at any time. She ran for the door and began to fiddle with the locks. But suddenly Sandy started to bark, and Annie heard footsteps on the stairs. She looked around wildly. There was nowhere to hide.

The phone! She should have thought of it sooner. She'd call Daddy Warbucks and tell him where she was. Annie picked up the receiver. But just then the door swung open. "Hang up," said a harsh voice. "Stop right where you are."

3
Rosie and Homer

There were two of them—a man and a woman. They looked nothing like the crooks Annie had seen in the movies and the comic strips. The woman was huge and wore a flowered housedress. Her stockings were rolled down, and she had on sturdy oxford shoes. The man was tall and stooped with a droopy walrus mustache. All his clothes hung on him as if they were meant for a much larger person. He was carrying two bags of groceries.

They almost crashed into each other trying to fit through the door. At last the woman pushed her way past and grabbed Annie. Sandy began to bark loudly.

"Tell your dog to quiet down," said the

woman. “We drugged him once to get him here, and we can do it again.” Her eyes were cold and vacant. Annie recognized the voice on the phone, but this time there was nothing motherly about it. “C’mon, Homer, grab the mongrel,” she directed.

“No, stop!” cried Annie. “Sandy, quiet down!”

Sandy could tell that Annie was serious. He stopped barking right away.

“Now get back on that chair,” the woman ordered. “Homer, tie her up.”

“No, you don’t have to do that,” said Annie, thinking fast. “I promise I’ll stay here. But what do you want with me? Why did you bring me here?”

“You might say we’re after a few of the better things in life, and you’re gonna help us get them,” said the woman.

“We’re sorry we had to kidnap you,” said the man meekly. “But it’s only for a while. We’ll give you a nice dinner, and then we’ll let you go just as good as new.”

“Homer, shut up! We weren’t gonna tell her we’d let her go, remember?”

"Aw, it can't do no harm," the man mumbled.

"My foot it can't!"

"But Rosie, the poor little thing must be scared stiff."

"That's the trouble with you, Homer. You always were too soft. And just look where it's gotten us. Well, I'm not gonna spend my old age in this dump, scrubbing floors that'll never get clean, climbing five flights of stairs—and me with my bad legs too."

Homer moved closer to his wife and patted her shoulder awkwardly. "Now, now, dear. There's no reason to get yourself upset. Remember your blood pressure."

As they talked Annie studied them. It was almost like Rosie was making Homer feel sorry for her so she could get her own way. Well, if it worked for Rosie, it could work for Annie just as well. Since Homer thought she was scared stiff, she'd try to act the part.

The truth was that Annie was too busy thinking to be scared. She'd been in plenty of tight spots before. There had to be a way out of this one. Rosie was a tough customer, no doubt about it, but Homer seemed like a pushover. The main thing was to stay on his good side and keep her eyes and ears open.

"I'm awful hungry," Annie said in a sad little voice. "Do you think I could have something to eat?"

Homer bustled over to the table and eagerly began to pull bread and sausages out of a bag of groceries. When Annie saw the meat, her stomach turned over. She felt like she couldn't eat a thing, but she was stalling for time. "Kidnap her," Homer had said. Annie knew kidnapping was a really bad crime; people went to jail for it. But she decided to play dumb so she could find out what Rosie and Homer were planning and just how far they were willing to go.

"Please," said Annie, looking as woeful as she could, "why don't you let me call my father? I know he misses me and Sandy something fierce. If you let us go, I'm sure he'll give you a reward."

"You bet he will!" Rosie snapped. "A million dollars worth of it. But you got the order all wrong. See, the way it works is that *first* he gives us the cash and *then* we let you go.

"Get over there now and pick up that phone. Call up Warbucks and tell him to take the ferry to the Statue of Liberty with one million dollars cash. Tell him to come alone. He has until midnight tonight. If the money isn't there, he can kiss his little girl good-bye."

Daddy Warbucks would be so frightened! They had some nerve using his love for her to get his money! Suddenly Annie's resolve to act like a poor unfortunate victim was forgotten. She drew herself up to her full height and looked Rosie Jiggs in the eye. "And if I refuse?" she said.

Rosie walked over to the sink, where her husband was making sandwiches. She took the carving knife out of his hand and advanced toward Sandy. "If you don't want to see your dog's throat slit, you'll pick up that phone right now. And I warn you, don't try any funny business."

Annie picked up the receiver. "Operator, operator, get me Oliver Warbucks. Yes, that's right. *The* Oliver Warbucks."

Daddy Warbucks answered on the first ring. "Where are you, Annie? Thank God, you're safe!"

Annie delivered the message. But at the end she quickly added, "Don't do it, Daddy! Don't give them the money!"

Rosie grabbed the phone. "She's alive now, Mr. Warbucks. But unless that money's left by the door of the Statue of Liberty at midnight, you'll never lay eyes on Annie again. And don't forget, you were told to come alone."

She hung up with a satisfied smile. "He's gonna do it, Homer. He's crazy about the little brat. The plan's gonna work. We'll be rich. Soon as we pick up the dough, we'll head straight for Mexico City. Ah, the beaches, the sunshine! Think of it, Homer, you'll never have to deliver milk again." She threw her arms around her husband and planted a loud kiss on his cheek.

This was Annie's chance. She decided

to make a run for it. There was nothing more to be gained by hanging around here. She bent down and whispered to Sandy, "Get her, boy!" As Sandy lunged for Rosie, Annie raced toward the door.

Just then Homer seemed to wake up. Very slowly he reached into his pocket and pulled out a pistol. "Not so fast," he said, pointing it at Annie. "Oh, dear, I was looking forward to fixing you dinner. I even had chocolate marshmallow cookies for your dessert. But now it looks like we might have to shoot you."

Annie gulped. She'd been wrong about Homer. He was quieter than his wife and maybe not so mean, but he was every bit as dangerous. For the first time a shiver of fear ran through her body.

Suddenly Sandy began to bark, and Annie heard a noise at the door as if someone were knocking very lightly. "Who could it be at this hour?" whispered Homer. "Maybe they'll go away."

Rosie grabbed Annie and put her hand over the girl's mouth. "I don't want to hear a sound out of you," she warned.

Tap, tap, tap. Tap, tap, tap. Whoever was at the door wasn't leaving. For a split second Annie thought that maybe Daddy Warbucks had traced her there. But no, if it were him he'd be pounding the door down.

Just then a soft little voice called out, "Hi, whatever your name is. I know you're in there. I've been watching from across the street, and you never came out. If you don't let me in, I'm gonna tell my mother. You should've came out by now."

It was Clara! What an amazing kid! Annie felt a rush of gratitude toward her. She wished she could tell her everything that was going on, but she was frightened of what Rosie and Homer might do.

"Get in the back room, Homer," Rosie whispered frantically. "Cover her with the gun. As for you, kid, go to the door and get rid of her. Say you'll be leaving right away. Remember, one false move and Homer'll blow you sky high."

Annie went to the door and unlocked it. There stood Clara with a big grin on her face. "Don't you think I was smart to find you?" she said. "Is this your dog? Gee, he's cute." Sandy thumped his tail on the floor. He knew a friend when he saw one.

"But what I want to know," Clara went on, "is why you're still here. See, I was waiting for you so I could walk back down the block with you. My house is right across the street, and I was waiting by the window. I guess I would've gotten tired of waiting, but you know what? There was some news on my mom's radio that a rich little girl was kidnapped, and they said she had red hair."

That's me! That's me! The words sounded in Annie's head, but she remembered how Homer had looked when he'd aimed the gun at her. She'd better not take any chances.

"Oh, that's not me," she said to Clara. "Didn't I tell you I grew up in an orphanage? Listen, Clara, I'm gonna be leaving here soon. But I'll come back and play with you sometime. Cross my heart."

"Okay," Clara said cheerfully. "My house is number 318. I live on the third

floor. I have some really swell games we can play with. See ya."

She waved at Annie and ran down the stairs. Homer rushed out from behind the curtain.

"What're we gonna do, Rosie? If it's on the news, you can bet the police are aftcr us. I knew I shouldn't have listened to you. Being a milkman would never have made us rich. But this life of crime ain't no picnic."

"Stop whining, Homer, you're giving me a headache. You know how I get when I have one of my migraines. Why, the last one went on for six days."

"My poor Rosie. I don't want you to worry, but we got ourselves a problem here. The cops are gonna be swarming all over the place, Rosie. They'll be at the bus depot, the train stations, all the airports. We'll never get out of the country alive."

In their panic Rosie and Homer had forgotten about Annie. She knelt down next to Sandy, concentrating with all her might. Perhaps there was a way to keep them from killing her and to prevent Daddy Warbucks from losing his hard-earned million at the same time. Rosie had said they were going to Mexico City. What if Annie were to go with them? And what if she could get a message to Daddy Warbucks so he would be waiting there with the police? Sandy—that was it! Sandy could carry a message.

Rosie's pocketbook was open on the drainboard. Casually Annie backed up to it and reached her hand behind her. She was in luck. Her fingers closed almost immediately around a fountain pen.

"Where's the bathroom?" she asked. "I really have to go."

"Back in there," said Rosie, gesturing toward the curtain. She wasn't even bothering to be nasty. Probably too worried about her own skin, Annie decided.

Five minutes later Annie came out of the bathroom and walked to the table where Rosie and Homer were talking. The note she'd written on toilet paper was rolled up in her dress pocket. "I can help you get away," she told them loudly.

"Fat chance!" jeered Rosie. "Don't make me laugh!"

Annie ignored her. "As it happens, Daddy Warbucks has his own autocopter, and he taught me how to pilot it. I'll make you a deal. If you promise to let me go once we get to Mexico City, I'll take you there in the autocopter. You can stop at the Statue of Liberty first and collect the million for your retirement."

Rosie's eyes lit up. "You know, it just might work," she said slowly to Homer. "Maybe the little brat isn't so dumb after all."

4
Airborne

Rosie grabbed her pocketbook and pushed Annie toward the door. "Quick, down the stairs," ordered Rosie. "And don't try anything smart. Keep in mind that Homer's got you covered and there are enough bullets here to take care of you *and* your mutt."

When they got to the building's entrance, Rosie stuck her head out the door. "It's okay, the coast is clear. Where's the truck parked, Homer?"

"Right around the corner, dear. Nothing to worry about."

All the lights in the buildings were out, and the city was quiet. It seemed really late. Annie hoped it was past midnight so that Daddy Warbucks would be back

from the Statue of Liberty. She had to get the message to him—it was her only chance.

The ride uptown in Homer's milk truck seemed to take forever. Homer was a pokey, careful driver. He stopped at every crosswalk and waited, even though there were no pedestrians on the streets. Annie was wild with impatience. Would she be able to tell Sandy what she wanted him to do once they reached the mansion? Would he be able to make a break for it?

At last Homer parked the milk truck, and they all got out. Annie led the way to the mansion.

"Some spread your daddy's got here," said Rosie. "Not bad, not bad at all. Now where did you say that autocopter was?"

"It's behind the house," Annie said. "Can't we just make a run for it?"

"Nothing doing," said Rosie harshly. "Warbucks' servants are probably posted at all the windows. Get down on your hands and knees and start crawling across the lawn. We'll be right behind you."

The mansion blazed with lights, but

Annie had no way of knowing whether or not Daddy Warbucks was inside. The grass was cold and wet with dew. In front of her the autocopter was a dark shape against the starry sky.

Annie stood up carefully and unlatched the side panel. Sandy jumped inside, and Rosie and Homer were about to follow. It was now or never! Annie reached into her pocket and clasped the note. She put it under Sandy's collar and then pushed him out of the cockpit. "Quick, Sandy!" she told him. "Take this to Daddy Warbucks. Go find Daddy!"

"Arf, arf!" barked Sandy, taking off across the lawn toward the back door.

Homer Jiggs shoved the gun in the small of Annie's back. "I knew we shouldn't have trusted her. Whose idea was this anyway?" he whined.

"Hers, you fool," said Rosie. "C'mon, kid, get this thing up in the air and make it snappy."

Annie looked at the instrument panel. She'd watched Punjab and Daddy Warbucks work the controls many times, but that was very different from doing it herself. "Hurry up, Daddy Warbucks," she prayed as she pushed the ignition button and pressed her foot on the gas.

The propeller began to revolve; the autocopter vibrated like a top. Then, through the windshield, she saw Sandy. A tall man was running after him. But it wasn't Daddy Warbucks—it was Punjab. Suddenly Rosie grabbed the throttle out of Annie's hand. The autocopter lurched forward and began to move across the lawn.

Homer opened the side panel and started shooting. Just in time Punjab grabbed Sandy and threw himself over

him onto the ground. Suddenly the autocopter rose up into the air. “The note!” screamed Annie. “Look under Sandy’s collar!” But she was not sure Punjab could hear her over the noise of the engine.

Daddy Warbucks’ mansion shrunk to the size of a little toy house and seemed to rock back and forth beneath them. “How do you steer?” yelled Rosie.

“Let her do it!” Homer yelled. He grabbed Annie’s hands and placed them on the throttle.

Rosie was breathing heavily. Beads of

sweat stood out on her forehead, and she looked slightly green. "You told us you could drive this thing—now drive it!" she ordered.

Annie pushed the throttle and moved the joy stick to steer them on course. She knew that to get to the Statue of Liberty they'd have to pass over the tops of the skyscrapers in midtown Manhattan. She checked the altimeter. They were flying far too low. They'd have to gain altitude—and fast!

The Empire State Building was already looming up before them. Which way was she supposed to move the throttle to bring them up? In desperation Annie pulled it toward her. But it was the wrong direction. Suddenly they dropped with a sickening thud. The Empire State Building was so close now that she could see desks and typewriters in the offices inside. "Push it away from you!" screamed Rosie.

"I know, I know," said Annie, pushing it hard. The autocopter began to rise. At last they cleared the signal tower with only inches to spare.

Annie took a moment to look down. She'd never gone up in the autocopter at night before. The city was spread below them like a jeweled carpet. Annie could see the lights of Broadway snaking diagonally across Manhattan.

"Keep your mind on your driving," warned Rosie. "Homer's trigger finger is getting itchy."

"Tell him to scratch it," Annie said. Rosie didn't scare her. What choice did they have but to keep her alive?

As they approached the vicinity of Wall Street, Annie looked into a mirror on the windshield, positioned to show the sky behind them. Her eyes widened in astonishment. Far back in the distance she could

see the lights of another helicopter. Had Punjab somehow managed to contact the police? Maybe she wouldn't have to go to Mexico City after all!

They began to cross over New York Harbor. The Staten Island ferry crawled slowly through the water, and Annie could see a giant ocean liner being pulled out to sea by three tugboats. Up ahead the Statue of Liberty stood with her torch raised, waiting for them. It was a place Annie had always wanted to visit, but she never imagined she'd be seeing it this way.

Annie was shocked by how small the island was. She peered through the windshield. There were sidewalks all around

the statue and a wide, clear area out in front. Annie calculated rapidly. This was where she'd land. She pulled on the throttle, and the autocopter dropped down. It was going to require split-second timing. She only hoped she could negotiate the landing without killing them all.

She checked the mirror again. Yes, the other helicopter was still there. She'd find out soon enough whether it was the police. Annie banked rapidly and moved the joy stick to the right. As she glanced down to check her ground points, she saw a tall, upright figure standing directly below them. It was Daddy Warbucks! Annie's mind flooded with horror. They'd crash right into him! He wouldn't have time to get away!

In a panic Annie reversed direction. The autocopter bounced hard on the ground and then hit the steps in front of the statue. She leaned on the joy stick with all her might, but it was too late. Flames streaked from the engine. A burst of fire illuminated the side of the building.

"We're burning!" screamed Rosie. "Abandon ship!" She reached across Annie and pulled the side panel open.

She and Homer climbed out of the cockpit and rushed to the edge of the water. But Annie sat still, numb with fear. Had she hit Daddy Warbucks? If he was dead because of the foolish risks she'd taken, there was no reason to go on living.

Smoke filled the cockpit. It got hotter and hotter, and there was the strong, choking smell of burning rubber. Annie slumped over the controls, uncaring. Suddenly she felt herself being pulled from the autocopter and out into the cool night air. Homer carried her gently to the sea wall and set her down.

"You always were a sucker for a sweet face, Homer," grumbled Rosie. "Now that you've saved her life, keep her covered with the gun. Personally I wouldn't trust that kid further than I could throw her."

The three of them stood there in silence as the autocopter burned. A wind came up and made the flames roar. Sparks shot from the windshield, and suddenly the *boom* of a huge explosion shook the island. Homer had not pulled Annie out a moment too soon.

But none of it mattered. She did not care that she was trapped with the Jiggses. She did not care that Homer still had a gun. It made no difference to her whether the police came or not. All Annie could think about was Daddy Warbucks.

At that moment a man was silhouetted briefly against the flames. His clothing was charred and he walked with a limp, but he was very much alive. Without even thinking of the gun jammed into her ribs, Annie ran toward him.

"Oh, Daddy Warbucks," she cried. "You're safe! You're safe!" As she fell sobbing into his arms, a single shot rang out.

5
The Showdown

"That's just a warning," said Rosie, marching toward them. "Homer's no saint, Warbucks, and he's running out of patience. You've got exactly thirty seconds to hand over the dough."

Annie didn't even stop to think. There was no way she'd let Daddy Warbucks give these crooks his money. "Don't do it, Daddy!" she yelled. "Don't tell them where it is!"

The next thing Annie knew, Rosie had slammed her to the ground, and Daddy Warbucks was bending over her. "How dare you strike my daughter!" he shouted at Rosie. "I'll have you put away for life."

Homer poked his gun into Daddy Warbucks' side, but he just slapped it away absent-mindedly. "Are you all right, Annie?" he asked. "She didn't hurt you, did she?" In the strange, smoky light his face was soft with concern.

Just then the high whine of an engine cut the air. A helicopter was landing on pontoons in the bay. Doors slammed and four heavily armed policemen climbed over the sea wall.

In a perfectly timed motion Homer grabbed Daddy Warbucks, and Rosie reached down and pulled Annie to her feet. "Stick up your hands, officer," Rosie ordered, "or we'll pump these suckers full of lead. Believe me, it would be a pleasure to do in this little brat. She's worse than a toothache on New Year's Eve."

Daddy Warbucks signaled to the policemen with a nod. "Back off, boys," he told them. "I won't have Annie's life put in jeopardy."

Rosie pushed Annie toward the sea wall. "You heard what the gentleman said. Now move aside, officers, and just keep walking. We're gonna have to borrow your helicopter. But first, Warbucks, hand over the dough."

Daddy Warbucks reached into his vest pocket and pulled out a wad of bills. "I'll give you anything you want. Just don't harm Annie," he said, handing it over.

"C'mon, kid, and you too, Pops, get inside that helicopter. We're taking a little ride, and you're doing the driving."

Uh-oh, thought Annie, it looked like it was all over. But she had forgotten about Punjab and Sandy. From behind the police helicopter two dark figures swam silently to the sea wall and emerged from the water.

With a low growl Sandy raced for Rosie. His teeth were bared and his body was taut as he hurtled toward her. Homer whirled around, holding out the gun. But it was too late. Punjab was waiting for him. With one quick karate chop he laid Homer out cold.

"Gee, Sandy, that was swell!" said Annie, hugging her wet, dripping dog. "I should have known I could count on you."

The police sergeant smiled at Annie

and shook her hand. "I want to congratulate you, little lady. I've been on the force for twenty years, but it's the first time I've ever seen a kidnap victim bring down her captors. Now I know you didn't plan that accident, but it sure gave us the time we needed. And if we hadn't arrived, the Mexican police would have been waiting for them south of the border."

"Aw shucks, officer, it was nothin'," said Annie. "Anyway, it was Punjab and Sandy who really caught Rosie and Homer. All I did was write a note and get them here." Remembering, she turned to Daddy Warbucks in dismay. "Oh, Daddy, your autocopter! I'm sorry I smashed it up."

Daddy Warbucks clasped Annie to him. "Forget the machine, Annie. We're both safe. That's the important thing. I would have given a million dollars–even a billion–to get you back. There's plenty more autocopters where that came from."

The police helicopter was still poised in the bay. Three policemen pushed and shoved the Jiggses toward it. Just before

she climbed over the sea wall, Rosie shook her fist at Annie and Daddy Warbucks. "All I can say is good riddance. Take the kid, Warbucks, and welcome to her. Jail's gonna be a relief after a day with that brat."

But Homer seemed downcast. He scuffed at the ground with his shoe and spoke in a voice low enough so that Rosie could not hear him. "Listen, girlie, I'm sorry. Really I am. I never wanted to do it. It was all the missus' idea. I kept tellin' her that bein' a milkman was good enough for us, but she wanted furs and jewels. Anyway, you're a brave little thing, and good luck to you and your old man."

The cop led Homer away, and he shuffled off without looking back again. Annie felt sorry for him. He should have stood up to Rosie. Maybe the only time he ever had was when he'd dragged Annie from the burning autocopter. She meant to tell Daddy Warbucks about that. She wondered if it would make any difference in what they did to Homer.

"Well, folks," said the sergeant. "We're taking these two down to the station and booking them for kidnapping. We'll send the coast guard cruiser back to pick you up as soon as we can radio them." The

police helicopter took off with its lights flashing and its siren blaring.

Soon the island was quiet once more. High above them the Statue of Liberty stood with her torch raised to welcome travelers. Annie looked all around her. Here were the people she loved. Near the sea wall Punjab was doing jumping jacks to keep warm. Sandy was wedged between Annie and Daddy Warbucks, getting them both soaking wet.

"C'mon, everyone," said Annie. "It's cozier around the fire." The four of them sat huddled near the smoldering autocop-

ter, thinking their own private thoughts. Finally Annie leaned against Daddy Warbucks with a sigh of contentment. "Gee, if only we had some marshmallows to roast. I sure could go for a cup of hot chocolate right about now."

Daddy Warbucks laughed and held her close. Far away in the distance they could see the green light of the coast guard cruiser moving across the water. They would soon be on their way home.